# SEA CHARACTERS

## Hal O. Graham

Holo Popups
Baltimore, Maryland
Copyright 2018

# SEA CHARACTERS

# How to use **Holo Popups**:

Follow these steps to bring these pages to life!

- Download the **Holo Popups** AR App from the App Store or Google Play.

- Turn on your sound and open the **Holo Popups** AR App.

- Point the spinning cursor at the pages with images.

- Watch as the pages are transformed into beautiful 3D animations.

- Save your photos & videos and share with your friends & family!

# Having trouble?  Here are a few things to try:

- Make sure the full image is in view (hold the phone 1-2 feet from the page).

- Flatten the pages if tracking is jumpy.

- Turn on the flash ⚡ in low lighting.

Email us at support@baltivirtual.com for help!

# Enjoy the magic of **Holo Popups!**

The animals living in the big blue sea

may look a bit different from you and me.

Some are big and others small.

Many swim, but a couple crawl!


The dolphin is known to be very smart,

and she moves through the waves like a work of art!

She plays with her friends - they all love to race,

and for lunch, she eats fish with her bottle-nosed face!

What's that there with two claws and eight feet?

Humans think it's quite the treat.

It has a shell so it doesn't become prey.

They're the blue crab at the bottom of the Bay!

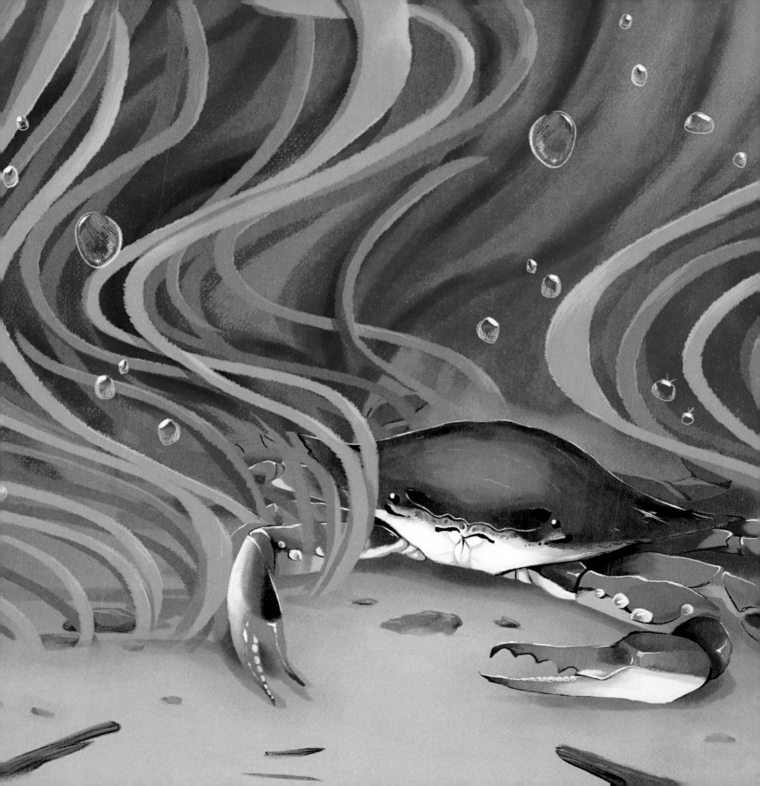

Look at these things - what marvelous creatures!

They have no eyes or facial features.

The jellyfish swim with beauty and grace,

but they might sting you if you get in their space!

The biggest sea predator is the killer whale -

he's longer than a bus from his nose to his tail.

He's not a fish, but a mammal like you,

and he comes to the surface to breathe air, too.

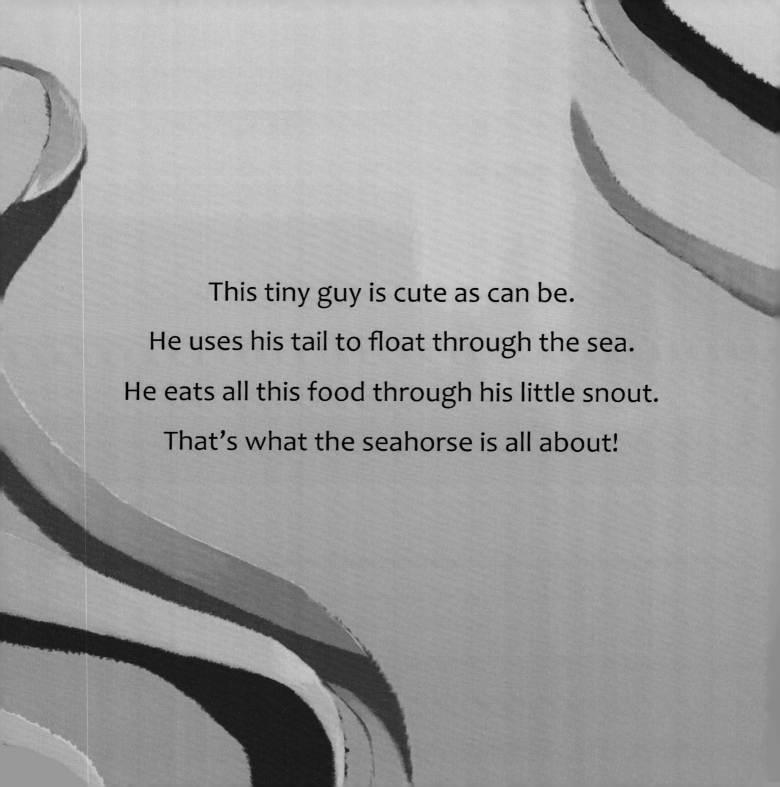

This tiny guy is cute as can be.

He uses his tail to float through the sea.

He eats all this food through his little snout.

That's what the seahorse is all about!

The sea turtle's shell is very tough -

to keep her safe if things get rough.

She goes to shore just once a year,

and after a week, her babies appear!

Who has eight arms and one head?

Is that an "octopus," you said?

It has no spine, but it's still very strong.

It uses suction cups to help it hang on.

With wide-set eyes she can see with ease.

The hammerhead views 360 degrees.

Alone she swims for most of her days,

eating up fish, squid, and stingrays!

The blue whale is the biggest creature on Earth -
it is already 25 feet at birth!
Biggest, and also the loudest too -
from 1,000 miles away you can hear Big Blue.


The salty sea is an interesting place.
We know less about it than we do about space.
We'll leave you with this final notion:
fish are our friends, so take care of the ocean!

**Holo Popups** is a publisher focused on augmented reality children's books. By bringing the best authors and the best animators together, we seek to create a uniquely magical experience for your child. Images on the pages come alive to entertain, educate, and energize your child. Books in the series appeal to a range of interests. They can be a part of your parent-child reading/bonding time as well as a cool, motivational tool for children to learn on their own.

**Hal O. Graham** was born and raised in Baltimore, Maryland. He spent his childhood reading pop-up books and has now moved on to developing augmented reality children's books. Hal wants your child's joy for reading to come to life just like the animations in his books. Hal loves science fiction, magic, and illusions. When not working on his latest children's book, Hal can be found hanging out with his virtual friends, created by the team at Holo Popups.

90124492R00015

Made in the USA
San Bernardino, CA
06 October 2018